# THE UGLY DUCKLING

PURPLE BEAR BOOKS · NEW YORK

# The Ugly Duckling

BY HANS CHRISTIAN ANDERSEN

ILLUSTRATED BY

ROBERTA ANGARAMO

IT WAS A BEAUTIFUL SUMMER DAY in the country. The cornfields were golden, the pastures green, the haystacks piled high in the meadows. Great forests grew all around the fields, and in the middle of these forests lay deep lakes. In a sunny spot at the top of a hill sat a stone castle and below it, along the riverbank, large bushes grew, and here sat a duck on her nest, waiting for her clutch of eggs to hatch. The duck was growing tired of the long wait and bored, too, since she seldom had visitors. The other ducks liked swimming in the river more than climbing the bank to talk with her.

At last, one shell cracked, and then another, and from each egg a duckling poked its head out and cried, "Peep, peep."

"Quack, quack," said the mother duck, and the ducklings scurried out of their shells as fast as they could and went peering about under the green bushes. The mother duck let them explore as much as they pleased, for green is good for the eyes.

"How large the world is!" said all the ducklings, for they had so much more room now than they'd had in their shells.

"Do you think that this is the whole world?" said the mother. "Wait until you have seen the garden. It stretches far away into that distant field." Then, turning to her brood, she asked, "Are you all here? No. The biggest egg has not hatched. I wonder how long it is going to be— I am getting so tired of it." Then she sat back down on the nest.

"How are you getting on?" said an old duck who stopped by.

"One egg has not hatched yet," said the mother duck. "It's taking such a long time. But just look at the others. Aren't they the prettiest little ducklings you ever saw?"

"Let me see that egg," said the old duck. "It may be a turkey's egg. I was once tricked into hatching some turkey eggs, and what a bother those young ones were! They couldn't swim at all. Yes, it must be a turkey's egg. You should leave it and teach the others to swim."

"Well," said the mother duck, "I've sat so long already, a few days more won't hurt."

At last the large egg cracked. "Peep! peep!" said the baby as he waddled out of the shell. Oh, how very large and ugly he was!

The mother duck looked at him. "This is a terribly big duckling," she said. "None of the others look like him. Maybe it really is a young turkey. Well, we shall soon see. Into the water he must go, even if I have to push him in myself."

The mother duck led her family down to the river and jumped in with a splash. "Quack, quack," she said, and one duckling after the other tumbled into the river after her. The water went over their heads, but they soon came up again and swam quite beautifully. They were all in the water, even the ugly gray duckling.

"No, this is not a turkey," said the mother duck. "See how nicely he uses his legs, how gracefully he carries himself. He is my own child and he is rather handsome when you look at him properly." Then she called to her children, "Quack, quack. Come along with me and I will take you into the world and introduce you to all the birds in the farmyard. Keep close to me so that no one steps on you and beware of the cat!"

As they entered the farmyard, the mother duck said, "Now use your legs, and make a nice bow to that regal old duck over here. Hurry up! Don't keep your feet together—a well-trained duckling turns its feet out—that's the way! Now bow and say 'quack.'"

And so they did, but all the other ducks in the farmyard looked at them, and said, "So now we are going to have this new lot, too—as if there were not enough of us already. Oh! Look at that ugly duckling— we don't want him here!" And one of the ducks flew at him and bit him on the back of the head.

"Let him alone," said the mother duck. "He's not doing you any harm."

"Those children of yours are very pretty," said the regal old duck. "All except that one."

"He is not pretty, but he is a very good child," said the mother duck. "And he swims beautifully—better than any of the others. I'm sure he will grow handsome in time, and no doubt he will get smaller. He has been lying too long in the egg. That is why his shape is not quite right." She scratched his neck and stroked him all over.

The other ducklings made themselves at home in the farmyard. But the poor ugly duckling was bitten, pushed, and sneered at both by the ducks and the hens. Every day it grew worse. The poor duckling was chased by everyone. His own brothers and sisters tormented him and kept saying, "If only the cat would get you, you silly thing!" Even the mother duck said, "If only you were far away!" The ducks bit him, the chickens pecked at him, and the girl who fed them kicked him.

The poor duckling was so miserable that one day he flew over the fence, frightening the little birds in the trees who flew off in a panic. It is because I am so ugly, thought the duckling. He ran until he came to the big moor where the wild ducks lived. Here he lay all night, feeling very tired and miserable. In the morning the wild ducks flew up and looked at the newcomer.

"Where do you come from?" they asked, and the duckling bowed politely to them as he'd been taught.

"How ugly you are!" said the wild ducks. "Just make sure you don't try to marry into our families."

Poor thing! He had no thought of getting married. All he hoped was that they'd allow him to lie in the rushes and drink a little water.

He lay there for two whole days, and then along came two wild geese, or rather wild ganders.

"Look here," they said, "you are so ugly that we have taken a fancy to you. Would you like to come along with us? On the next moor there are some lovely wild geese. Even though you are so ugly, one of them might like you."

*Bang! Bang!* sounded in the air. The two ganders fell down dead in the rushes. Again the sound—*Bang! Bang!*—and the whole flock of wild geese flew up from the reeds. Then there was another bang. It was a large shooting party and the hunters lay all around the moor. The blue smoke rose in clouds through the dark trees and floated away across the water.

Then splashing through the mud came the dogs, bending reeds and rushes on all sides. The poor duckling was terribly frightened.

Just as he turned his head to hide it under his wing a huge dog stood before him, his tongue hanging out of his mouth and his wild eyes glowering. He thrust his nose close to the duckling, showing his sharp teeth, and then *splash!* Away he went without touching him.

"Oh! Heaven be thanked!" sighed the poor duckling. "I am so ugly that even the dog would not eat me." And he lay quite still, while the shots were whizzing among the reeds as the hunters fired again and again.

It was late in the day before things began to get quiet, but the poor duckling did not dare move. He waited for several hours, then he hurried away from the moor as fast as he could. Over fields and meadows he ran, but it was so windy, he found it difficult to make much progress. Toward evening he reached a humble little cottage. It was so dilapidated that it didn't know which way to fall, so it remained standing.

The wind was whistling so hard that the duckling had to sit down in order not to be blown away. The weather was getting worse. Suddenly he noticed that the door of the cottage had broken away from its hinges and was hanging so crookedly that he could just creep through the crack. That is what he did.

An old woman lived there with her cat and her hen. The cat, called Sonny, could arch his back and purr and could even give out sparks if you stroked his fur the wrong way. The hen had small stumpy legs and therefore was called Chick-a-biddy Shortshanks. She laid plenty of eggs, and the old woman loved her like her own child.

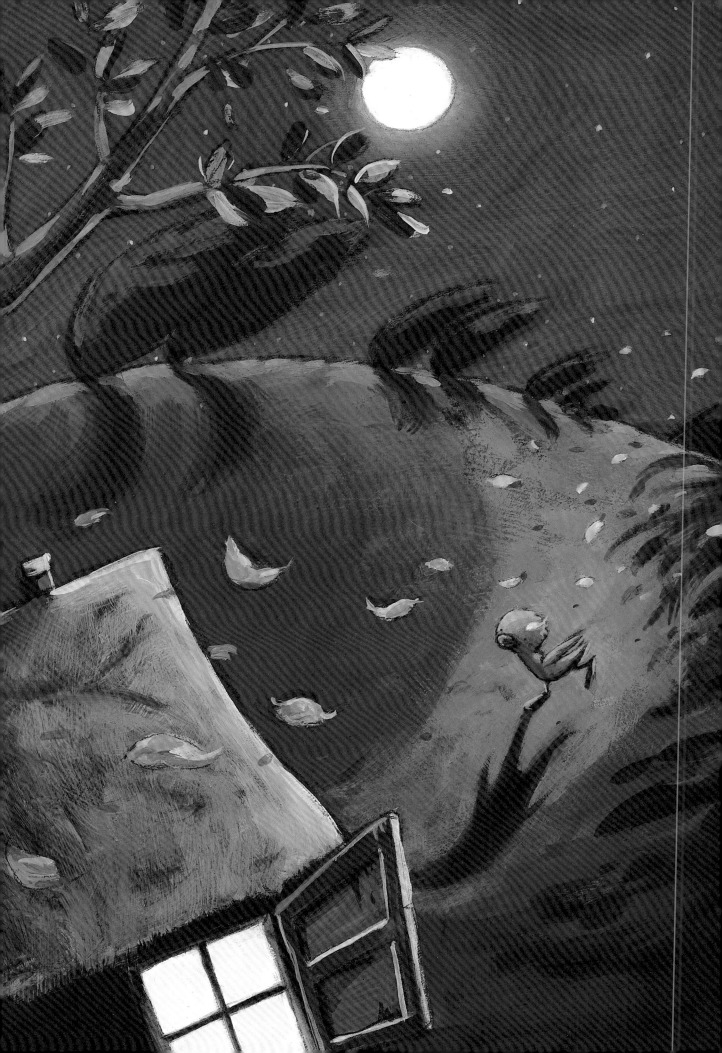

In the morning, they immediately discovered the strange duckling. The cat began to purr and the hen to cackle.

"What is the matter?" said the old woman, peering around, but since she did not see well, she thought that the duckling was a fat duck that had gone astray. This is a great find, she thought. Now I shall have duck's eggs, if only it is not a drake. So the duckling was put on trial for three weeks, but he didn't lay a single egg.

The cat was master of the house and the hen was mistress, and so they always said, "We and the world," for they considered that they were half the world, and the better half. The duckling thought that others might have a different opinion, but the hen disagreed. "Can you lay eggs?" she asked. "No. Well, then, hold your tongue!"

And the cat said, "Can you arch your back, or purr, or give out sparks? No. Well then you aren't allowed to have an opinion." So the duckling sat in a corner, most depressed. Then he began to think of fresh air and sunshine and felt a strange longing to be on the water. He had to tell the hen about it.

"Do you know what's the matter with you?" she said. "You have nothing to do—that is why you get such a silly idea into your head. If you could lay an egg or purr, you would forget about such things."

"But it is so lovely to swim on the water," said the duckling, "to feel the water close over your head when you dive down to the bottom!"

"Lovely?" said the hen. "You must be crazy! The cat is clever. Ask him if he likes to swim. The old woman is wise. Ask her if she likes to dive down under the water."

"You don't understand me," said the duckling.

"Just be thankful for all we've done for you. You're lucky to be in this warm house."

"I think I will go out into the wide world," said the duckling.

"Do as you please!" said the hen.

So the duckling went.

He floated on the water and dived beneath it, but everywhere he went, the other animals avoided him because of his ugliness.

Autumn came, the leaves in the forest turned yellow and brown, and the wind took hold of them and made them dance about.

The air turned very cold and the clouds were heavy with snow. A raven stood shivering on a stone wall, crying, "Caw! Caw!" Just thinking about winter was enough to make one feel frozen, and the

poor duckling certainly had a very bad time of it.

One evening as the sun was setting, a flock of large beautiful birds rose out of the bushes. The duckling had never seen anything so lovely as these birds, so shining white with long, slender necks. They were swans. They gave an extraordinary cry as they spread their magnificent wings and flew away from this cold country to warmer lands across the wide seas.

As they rose high, high in the air, a strange feeling came over the ugly duckling. He whirled round and round, stretched his neck up after them, and let out a cry so loud and strange that he frightened himself. Ah! He could not forget those beautiful birds! He loved them as he had never loved anyone else. He didn't envy them—how could he ever dream of such loveliness for himself? He would be grateful if only the ducks would put up with him, poor ugly thing that he was.

The winter grew colder and colder. The duckling had to keep swimming day and night to keep the water from freezing. But every day the hole in which he swam grew smaller. At last he was so exhausted that he gave up and lay still. And soon he froze fast into the ice.

Early in the morning a peasant came along and saw him. He knocked a hole in the ice and took him home to his wife. And there they revived him. The children wanted to play with him, but the duckling was afraid and in a panic fluttered into the milk basin, spilling the milk all over the floor. The woman screamed and clapped her hands in the air. More frightened than ever, the duckling flew down into the butter tub and from there to the flour barrel. What a sight he was! The woman chased him, and the children, laughing and shouting, tried to catch him. Luckily the door was open, so the poor frightened duckling ran out of the house and hid in the bushes, collapsing exhausted on the newly fallen snow. It would be too sad to tell of all the misery he suffered during that long, hard winter.

One day the sun again began to shine warmly. The larks were singing. Spring had come! The duckling sat in a large garden where apple trees bloomed and sweet-scented lilac blossoms hung down over the river. Suddenly through the thicket came three beautiful white swans, floating gently on the water. The duckling recognized the beautiful creatures and was overcome by a strange feeling of sadness. I will fly over to those royal birds, and they will peck me to death because I,

who am so ugly, dare to approach them, he thought. But it is better to be killed by them than to be bitten by the ducks, pecked by the chickens, kicked by the farm girl, and suffer misery all winter. So he swam toward the beautiful swans. "Kill me!" said the duckling, and bent his head to the water, awaiting death. There he saw his own image, but he was no longer an ugly gray bird. He was a swan! It doesn't matter if you are born in a duck yard as long as you are hatched from a swan's egg.

The swans swam around him and stroked him with their beaks. Into the garden came some little children, and the smallest of them cried, "Look! There is a new one!" And the other children shouted, "Yes, yes! And he is by far the prettiest!"

And the old swans bowed to him. He was so happy, but not at all proud, for a good heart is never proud. Then he rustled his feathers, curved his slender neck, and cried joyfully from the depths of his heart, "I never dreamed of so much happiness when I was the ugly duckling!"

Illustrations copyright © 2005 by Roberta Angaramo

First published in Taiwan in 2005 by Grimm Press

First English-language edition published in 2006 by Purple Bear Books Inc., New York.

Adapted from the translation by W. Angeldorff

For more information about our books, visit our website: purplebearbooks.com

Library of Congress Cataloging-in-Publication Data is available.

This edition prepared by Cheshire Studio.

TRADE EDITION

ISBN-10: 1-933327-09-X

ISBN-13: 978-1-933327-09-9

1 3 5 7 9 TE 10 8 6 4 2

LIBRARY EDITION

ISBN-10: 1-933327-10-3

ISBN-13: 978-1-933327-10-5

1 3 5 7 9 LE 10 8 6 4 2

Printed in Taiwan